D1539837

A Note to Parents and Caregivers:

Read-it! Readers are for children who are just starting on the amazing road to reading. These beautiful books support both the acquisition of reading skills and the love of books.

 The PURPLE LEVEL presents basic topics and objects using high frequency words and simple language patterns.

 The RED LEVEL presents familiar topics using common words and repeating sentence patterns.

 The BLUE LEVEL presents new ideas using a larger vocabulary and varied sentence structure.

 The YELLOW LEVEL presents more challenging ideas, a broad vocabulary, and wide variety in sentence structure.

 The GREEN LEVEL presents more complex ideas, an extended vocabulary range, and expanded language structures.

 The ORANGE LEVEL presents a wide range of ideas and concepts using challenging vocabulary and complex language structures.

When sharing a book with your child, read in short stretches, pausing often to talk about the pictures. Have your child turn the pages and point to the pictures and familiar words. And be sure to reread favorite stories or parts of stories.

There is no right or wrong way to share books with children. Find time to read with your child, and pass on the legacy of literacy.

Adria F. Klein, Ph.D.
Professor Emeritus
California State University
San Bernardino, California

Editor: Christianne Jones
Page Production: Melissa Kes/JoAnne Nelson
Art Director: Keith Griffin
Managing Editor: Catherine Neitge
The illustrations in this book were rendered in watercolor.

Picture Window Books
5115 Excelsior Boulevard
Suite 232
Minneapolis, MN 55416
877-845-8392
www.picturewindowbooks.com

Printed in the United States of America.

All books published by Picture Window Books
are manufactured with paper containing at least
10 percent post-consumer waste.

Library of Congress Cataloging-in-Publication Data
Blackaby, Susan.
Meg takes a walk / by Susan Blackaby ; illustrated by Sharon Holme.
p. cm.—(Read-it! readers)
Summary: In simple sentences, tells about the adventures that occur when Meg takes her
dog Peg for a walk.
ISBN-10: 1-4048-1005-6 (hardcover)
ISBN-13: 978-1-4048-1005-1 (hardcover)
ISBN-10: 1-4048-1208-3 (paperback)
ISBN-13: 978-1-4048-1208-6 (paperback)
[1. Dogs—Fiction. 2. Walking—Fiction.] I. Holme, Sharon, ill. II. Title. III. Series.

PZ7.B5318Me 2004
[E]—dc21   2004019175

Meg Takes a Walk

By Susan Blackaby
Illustrated by Sharon Holme

Special thanks to our advisers for their expertise:

Adria F. Klein, Ph.D.
Professor Emeritus, California State University
San Bernardino, California

Susan Kesselring, M.A.
Literacy Educator
Rosemount-Apple Valley-Eagan (Minnesota) School District

CANCEL

PiCTURE WiNDOW BOOKS
Minneapolis, Minnesota

Meg takes Peg for a walk.

Peg turns right when Meg turns left.

Meg tugs the leash.

Mr. Reed is fixing a bird feeder.
Meg helps.

Peg helps, too. Meg tugs the leash.

Mrs. Perry is picking berries.

Meg helps.

Peg helps, too. Meg tugs the leash.

Bill is selling snow cones. Meg helps.

Peg helps, too. Meg tugs the leash.

Kitty is stuck in a tree. Meg helps.

Peg helps, too. Meg tugs the leash.

Oh no! There goes Kitty!

Oh no! There goes Peg!

Kitty runs past Mrs. Perry.

Peg spills the berries.

Kitty runs past Mr. Reed.

Peg tips the bird feeder.

Kitty runs past Bill.

Peg spills the snow cones.

Meg helps clean up the mess.

Peg doesn't help.

Peg takes a nap. She's had a
very busy day.

More *Read-it!* Readers

Bright pictures and fun stories help you practice your reading skills.
Look for more books at your level.

Allie's Bike
Busy Bear
Caleb's Race
Danny's Birthday
Fable's Whistle
Goldie's New Home
Jake Skates
New to Drew
Riley Flies a Kite
The Traveling Shoes
Tricia's Talent
A Trip to the Zoo
Willy the Worm

On the Web

FactHound offers a safe, fun way to find Web sites
related to topics in this book. All of the sites on FactHound
have been researched by our staff.

1. Visit *www.facthound.com*

2. Type in this special code:
   1404810056

3. Click on the FETCH IT button.

Your trusty FactHound will fetch the best sites for you! A complete
list of *Read-it!* Readers is available on our Web site:
www.picturewindowbooks.com

24